From Death

© Copyright © Meredith Tucker

Chapter On

My name is Anita O'Connell. This is the story of my life, from my childhood and how I grew up into the woman that met Michael Doyle, to the woman that is now leaving Second-Phase and entering a new lease of life.

The year is 2420. It's a bright day in spring, where the air is sweet. I want to explain many things that are important to understand. I have recently left my digital afterlife in Second-Phase. I died one hundred years ago of old age, at the age of 116.

I remember entering Second-Phase. It really is the most amazing place. A digital world that feels, smells and tastes as rich as the real world. Yet with a click of one's phone coordinates, you can be teleported onto another planet beyond the scope of the things you have seen on Earth. In Second-Phase, there are many versions of Earth to enter – which are called 'printouts' – that are made every ten years.

    Michael and I had always planned that when we died, we would make our home in one of the imagined worlds of Second-Phase. We would live somewhere hot, with a great flowing beach surrounding our home.

    I died before Michael; he lived till he was 140. A good age. Scientists have created medicines which help slow down the aging process. There are also so many health advancements, which mean diseases are so much easier to treat than they were once upon a time.

    I know of people who had cancer eradicated from their bodies in a matter of days with the lightning-fast chemo advancements and medicine. There is a special form of nano-surgery, which means micro-robots can get rid of cancerous cells. I love science! It has liberated the human race.

    Michael and I never had any children. My sister had two daughters, whom I had a close relationship with. I would always send them birthday presents and call them every now and then. I was close with my sister Bethanie, and this was something that had always been a big part of my life.

I remember when I died officially. I recall entering Second-Phase because of the chip implanted in me so long ago. I remember how when I entered, I was guided through the process.

Once I was accustomed to the reality and the strange way I felt like myself again, one of the first things I did was make myself look young again. I booked a session with a doctor and filled out the forms to be in this digital existence as I had been at the age of thirty.

I remember how I did that having been in Second-Phase for only a matter of days. I had seen the interviews with people on television, explaining how it was lovely to be young again.

I recall looking in the mirror after the doctor had completed the procedure. All he had to do was ask me a bunch of questions and type certain things into his computer. Then I slept for what felt like a day and the next thing I knew, I woke up in the youthful body I had possessed in my thirties.

The reason I did not pick the body of my twenties was because I had met Michael in my early thirties. We had both decided we would look this way in Second-Phase.

I call still remember how wonderful it was to feel and look thirty again. I had the long brown hair and bright eyes that had once belonged to me. My body was the same size, as I wanted to look exactly the same as I had when Michael and I had met. I was about a UK dress size twelve when we had met and this is what my averagely slender figure looked like when my body was rejuvenated in Second-Phase.

After the doctor's appointment, I remember going home to the house in the imagined worlds which Michael and I had agreed I should buy as our home. He was still an elderly man in the real world.

I remember calling him on the video chat, seeing his face light up as he looked at me. An image of the woman he had fallen in love with.

*****

Yet this isn't the story of my life in Second-Phase, an adventure that was as rich as my life on Earth. This is the story of how I left Second-Phase one hundred years later; how I re-entered Earth and started a new life.

Michael and I spent around a hundred years in Second-Phase together. During this time, we travelled to many places in the digital realm. We achieved a lot. We felt as sensual as we had done in life. We chose to always be in our thirties: young, attractive and in a world full of joy.

Yet over the years, our marriage began to decay. What had made me love him was still present, yet neither of us were in love with each other anymore.

We had spent our lives together and now a digital afterlife of nearly one hundred years as well.

I remember it was Michael who expressed how he wanted a divorce. He said the words kindly, and I did not cry because I felt the same.

Michael had been the love of my life. I remember meeting him at a university party and falling in love with his quiet beauty and soft, gentle manners.

I still remember how he introduced himself. How he was wearing a yellow jumper and his blond curly hair framed his face.

Yet that was a lifetime ago. Michael and I had already experienced countless joys in our lives together. So, when we divorced, I was OK with it. We had experienced over a hundred years of marriage together, after all!

'I'm leaving Second-Phase,' Michael had said to me, as we discussed the logistics of our divorce. 'I want to be one of the first generations of people to enter one of the habitable planets.'

I remember the shock I felt, knowing Michael wanted to enter one of those planets. The robots had been preparing the five planets for many years. The shuttles were taking people from

Second-Phase to be reanimated in their bodies once the ship arrived on the planets.

There were five planets and Michael had selected the one closest to Earth to start a new life on. All of the planets were safe to live on. Yet he would be part of the first generation of people to exist on the planet. He would be a founding member.

I knew this was not what I wanted for myself. I wanted to leave Second-Phase finally and re-enter Earth. The technology had advanced so much. I was fortunate that the technology to do this had been developed while I was alive on Earth, so that I could now enter Earth once more in the body I knew well. My body could be created from sample tissue that was frozen in the vaults.

So, Michael and I were going to go our separate ways. I was to enter Earth once more and Michael was leaving for the planet Veranna.

We would never see each other in person again. The robots had already started the program, so a Second-Phase existence awaited the people of the five habitable planets, yet their Second-Phases were not connected to the program on Earth, although it was an exact copy of the technology. So, this meant when Michael died once again after a long life on Veranna, I would never see him on Earth's digital afterlife platform, as he would be in the digital afterlife of Veranna.

    I would soon be leaving Second-Phase, as would my dear ex-husband Michael, yet we were on completely different journeys for the next stages of our life.

*****

I knew that I would re-enter Earth in a copy of the same body that had belonged to me all my life. The prospect of soon inhabiting a body like that which I had known vividly in the Second-Phase reality was exciting.

    I had requested that I re-enter Earth in the printed body that was how I had been aged twenty. The body would inhabit my chip and my mind would be downloaded into it. It would be fully organic and able to produce children. It would be my body and it would age as every other human's body does.

I had signed the papers and requested that when the body died naturally – as I had died once before – that I would return to Second-Phase to continue living on in the digital afterlife.

Science had improved and my doctors estimated that because of the fact that I died aged 116, in today's modern times I could expect to live to 160 with the aid of medication.

My sister Bethanie, my mum and dad, my grandparents and the rest of my family were to remain in Second-Phase. I was one of a group of people entering as the first generation to re-enter a human body after being in Second-Phase.

It was like coming back from the dead, except Second-Phase feels as much like life on Earth did in how vivid it is. Second-Phase is as real an experience as life was.

My ex-husband Michael would still be in digital form. He was part of a group of people from Second-Phase who would go on to bring up the first generation of children to be born on the planet Veranna.

It would take Michael twenty-five years to reach Veranna. The robotic team had already built the cities and cloned animals to flourish on the planet.

We no longer loved each other romantically. I don't think that people can stay in love for all eternity. I think human relationships are not meant to last that long. Before Second-Phase, we would die at death, yet now the possibilities were endless.

*****

Michael was part of a group of twelve million citizens from Second-Phase who would guide the first generation of babies on the planet.

He had already agreed to bring up one child who was born from the sperm and egg donation of a relative of his still on Earth. He would bring the child up as if it were his own, when in fact he was a great, great, great grandfather of the baby.

'I will tell the child this truth. I will give it all the love I have to give,' he said, as he described to me his plan.

'You will be such an amazing dad to the child,' I said.

Michael looked at me with a soft and kind expression. His blue eyes lit up as he described his excitement for Veranna.

'It looks such a beautiful planet from the photos. The nearest of the five habitable worlds. It will be twenty-five years from now, yet when you get there, please send me an email about your life,' I said to him.

'Of course. I know we are no longer married, yet you will always be a cherished friend of mine,' Michael said, with kindness in his voice.

*****

Michael's mission to leave for Veranna meant that he left Second-Phase before I did. We no longer lived in the same house together. I still lived in the imagined worlds, yet he had moved back to a printout of Earth from the time when he had died a physical death.

He sent me a Facebook message on the day that he was to leave for Veranna. I replied wishing him all the best.

It was a televised event; as the twelve million citizens from all around Second-Phase were uploaded into the information systems, they disappeared from Second-Phase and entered a system which would carry them in a sleep state to Veranna.

I would only hear from him in twenty-five years' time, for he would be asleep. It would only feel like a moment had passed for him since leaving Second-Phase and entering the huge planet of Veranna, which was larger than Earth in size.

I watched the television presenter from Second-Phase describe this momentous day, that what was labelled as 'generation zero' would bring up 'generation one', the first people to live on the planet Veranna.

In three months' time, the next mission was taking place for a further twelve million citizens of Second-Phase to leave that reality and take a mission for the second habitable planet, Sueno – which meant 'dream' in Spanish. It was the name chosen by the Spanish astronomer who had discovered the planet.

There were five of these missions in total and the human race would live on in the five habitable planets. They would receive communications from Earth, yet the human race would also continue to exist further into the universe. All of these planets were in our universe.

I remember watching the television presenter describe the momentous event of people leaving for Veranna. She was blonde and tall. She was obviously as excited as everyone else was.

'Today is one of those momentous days in human history. Today we go forth to live on other planets,' she beamed.

I enjoyed watching the celebrational television broadcast. Michael was in the spaceship which had left for Veranna. I had already set a date in my phone for twenty-five years' time, when I would next hear from him.

We still had each other on Facebook. His Facebook colours had changed to the orange which indicated someone had left for the habitable worlds. Mine was currently green, which indicated that I was in Second-Phase, yet it would soon turn purple to indicate that I was a person re-entering Earth from Second-Phase. Blue was the colour for all social media which indicated a person was in their first life on Earth and yet to die.

Chapter Two

I remember preparing to leave Second-Phase. I looked through my forms and I had been there for exactly 102 years! That is a long time.

In that time, I had spent most of it married to Michael. We had divorced five years previously yet still remained friends.

I woke up in the imagined world of Freedom, which was a whole planet created in digital reality as part of Second Phase. Michael and I had lived there all of our lives together in Second-Phase.

I had left the house which we owned together. I had moved to a one-bedroom flat that was part of a high complex overlooking a beach. In Second-Phase, everything runs on a micro-economy. Properties are the price of shampoo in the real world.

I remember buying my flat in Freedom when Michael and I were getting divorced. The divorce was simple; we already had separate bank accounts. We did have one joint account – that we had previously used to donate money to charities – which we emptied and closed.

My property cost me £1. In Second-Phase, you are only allowed one property at a time. The most money anyone can take is £1,000,000 of British money with them when they enter Second-Phase.

Yet everyone gets a benefit of around £10 a week. Now, when you think that a pleasant flat costs £1, you can imagine that money is no problem.

I digress a little, it's just these things are important to understand what life was like in Second-Phase.

I was soon to be going back to the real world. I could already feel and taste things in this reality just as vividly as I had done in my life.

I joined a Facebook group for Second-Phase residents who were re-entering Earth. The group was the generation of 2400s who were coming back to Earth to reside in London.

I had already filled out the forms and organised that I would wake up in Northwick Park Hospital as a twenty-year-old, looking the same as I have always looked, because my new body would be made from the DNA samples stored in the vaults.

I joined the group in search of new friends who I could meet up with prior to leaving Second-Phase. I hit it off with a woman called Charlotte.

She had been in Second-Phase for longer than I had. She had chosen to look different from her natural body, telling me how she had been a 'plain Jane' in her life on Earth.

Charlotte was really friendly and outgoing. She had long blonde hair and electric blue eyes. She was very slender and spoke with a loud, overly dramatic voice. We had met a few days after talking, knowing that we would both be starting a new chapter in our lives in London.

We met in the most modern printout of London, in a quiet pub called the Green Orchard. The latest printout was done this year, as they were printed every ten years.

Charlotte was wearing a beautiful flared purple dress. Her long, white-blonde hair was curled. She smiled when she saw me.

'Anita, hi.'

'It's good to meet you,' I said.

'I know right,' she replied, hugging me, and I could smell her floral perfume.

Charlotte and I discussed how we were both being brought back in London. We had talked about hobbies and interests, yet we both shared details on our Facebook profiles about our education and hobbies, so we both could see a lot about each other.

Charlotte was going to be living in Camden when she re-entered Earth. She was originally from America in her life on Earth and had wanted to live in England for the adventure.

'What will you do in Harrow?' she asked me, as she sat in the pub with a glass of red wine.

'I don't know yet. All my family will be behind in Second-Phase. My mum thinks I should look for a new man.'

'Oh, agreed! Me too. But not straight away,' Charlotte said, beaming. 'How old is your body meant to be, mid-twenties?'

'No, I'm based on the body I had in life. The body you will see me in when I am back on Earth, I was thirty when I looked like this.'

'Oh! Lucky you. Well, you have seen my pictures. You know I looked nothing like this in my life.'

'You were lovely,' I said with a smile, and it was true. She looked like a film star as I looked at her in the quiet pub, yet in her life on Earth she was small and plain.

'Thank you, thank you, darling. But no – I will reinvent myself. I've ordered a beautiful mould to live my life out. Will start as a fresh twenty-year-old and age gracefully!'

You could have a body made up for you by modern science that would harbour your mind; it would be made from cell tissue. They had catalogues for people re-entering Earth to choose bodies that suited them.

'Would you mind showing me a picture if you have one of the body you chose, so I know what you'll look like?' I ask.

Charlotte gets out her phone and shows me an image of a photo of a girl in a white vest with flowing black hair and amazing blue eyes.

'I'm the third person leaving Second-Phase to choose that model. One's someone on Earth and the other's going to the planet Sueno.'

'Wow, so someone else on Earth will look exactly like you,' I say, feeling a little awkward.

'Yes, darling. But there will only be one me,' said Charlotte, beaming.

We ordered food from the pub. We sat on a table together and talked about what we would do in London. We really got on well and I was glad that I had made a friend who I would be able to meet with back on Earth.

After the food, we had one more drink and took a few selfies together, which we posted on Instagram.

'Next time we meet, it will be on Earth. Not long now,' Charlotte said with a smile, her blue eyes a similar colour to the ones that were to be a part of the body she had chosen.

'I look forward to getting to know you more. Shall we go to the cinema when we get settled in?'

'Fine. Sounds perfect. See you soon, love,' Charlotte said.

Charlotte hugged me and then typed in the coordinates to go back to her home. As her watch beeped, she disappeared.

I sat in the pub for a little while longer. The barmaid smiled at me from across the bar. She was robotic staff and not an actual human. The robotic barmaid looked completely human and beautiful with her purple hair.

I would be entering Earth in a few weeks. I was excited. I would miss Second-Phase. I would miss the endless worlds and the ability to teleport home.

Yet Earth awaited me! The real world where I was born. A place where I not only had the possibility of finding love but possibly could even have a child. Or if not, I could get a dog! God, I had missed real dogs. Robotic dogs that imitated what a real dog did were wonderful, yet they were only designed so that people don't miss real animals too much. Animals were not allowed to enter Second-Phase. When they died, they died and went to heaven beyond this Earth.

I looked at my phone. It was a big Samsung Android device. I saw that Charlotte had sent me a little note on Facebook Messenger saying how nice it was to have met me.

I put my phone away. I'm always careful of my phone even though in Second-Phase one can't lose their phone. It's part of their digital code. Yet it's good that I'm careful because in the real world phones are made of physical material.

I typed in the coordinates to go back to Freedom and my flat there. My one-bedroom flat had an open-plan design. A few pictures from interesting artists decorated the living room.

I poured myself a cup of tea and snuggled up on the yellow sofa. I turned the TV on. Channels from the real world and Second-Phase all belonged to my television. There were paid services such as independent channels or Netflix, etc.

I watched the news for my city in the world of Freedom. On it they talked about the general economy on the particular news programme which I had switched over to.

As I drank my tea, I thought of how soon I'd be leaving my flat that I'd lived in for five years. Soon I'd be leaving the imagined world of Freedom, where Michael and I had spent over a hundred years together in.

I imagined how he was now asleep. In twenty-five years, he would wake in Veranna. He would be a dad and soon after he had assimilated to the world and the print of his body, he would have a son grow in an artificial womb. He had chosen to bring up a boy. I wondered if he would have biological children as well. I wondered if he would meet someone.

His son would be part of generation one of the world of Veranna. Michael is what is described as a generation zero, as he comes from Second-Phase on Earth.

Chapter Three

I meet with my sister and parents. My sister Bethanie has two daughters who went on to have children of their own.

We have a special app where we trace the generations on Earth. We like to support them emotionally in their lives, as most families do with their kin.

I love seeing Bethanie. We go to a restaurant and spend time with my parents.

'This will be the last time you're here for so long,' my mum says; she is crying but is smiling.

'I know, Mum, I know.'

'It's exciting, I know. It's just weird. You're still my baby in my heart.'

The restaurant we go to is one of my favourites in the town of Heva that I live in within Freedom. It's just by the beach and you can see the pink sky overlooking the surroundings and the people enjoying themselves.

The glass design of the restaurant means we can watch the world go by as we dine. We eat a chicken dish. Of course, no actual meat really exists in Second-Phase. It's all artificial and part of the digital reality that exists on the very complex computer system on Earth.

'Will you become a vegetarian again on Earth?' Mum asks.

'No, Mum. But you know I'll only eat lab-made meat,' I say with a smile as I take a sip of my lemonade.

'Yes, that's right. It's cheaper anyway,' my mum says, smiling.

We enjoy our meal and talk about many things. We remember our lives together on Earth: the house we lived in. Dad takes some pictures on his phone of the four of us together.

When we part and all teleport back home, I feel strange. I will be on my own out there in the world. One hundred years has passed since I was a little old lady on Earth. I will have almost everyone I love back in Second-Phase. I know that it's going to be OK. I can talk with them whenever I want, yet it will not be the same when I can't smell them and touch them.

*****

Over the next few days, I go for walks along the beach in Freedom. I look through my computer, which I will have a copy of when I enter Earth.

I have done a lot in my time in Second-Phase. I studied Graphic Design at a college here in Freedom. I did the equivalent of a Level 3 diploma. I worked as a graphic designer making logos and book covers for people on Earth and in Second-Phase.

I worked freelance on a site called Fiverr. Yet I also worked for a company where I had an office and a work computer. I would sit at my desk and design colourful logos for businesses.

When I got home each day from my work at the office, I would spend time with Michael. We would watch films or play sports. We had such an enjoyable life in Second-Phase.

I worked two days a week at that office. I worked there for twenty-five years. I never decided to do a degree in Graphic Design and thus I never got promoted. Yet money isn't an issue in Second-Phase, so work really was for the enjoyment of it.

Like I said, I also did freelance work designing logos and book covers on Fiverr. My employer knew about this and thought it was great.

I really enjoyed making book covers especially. I didn't bother to read the books that I designed covers for, as I made a lot of covers and have never been a huge reader. I prefer TV and films. Yet I did enjoy my freelance work just as much as my office job.

I would sit in our home where me and Michael lived. On my laptop, I would use photoshop and the chosen stock image that the client had selected to make amazing covers.

I charged £12 for a book cover for Kindle, audiobook and paperback. It was a good price and meant indie authors around the world could use my services.

A lot of people interested in writing would have ghostwriting programs. Which were artificial intelligence (AI) writing packages that write them a book once they have described the plot and answered the required questions. If a book was written by an AI ghostwriting package, it had to be mentioned on the cover.

When Michael and I divorced, I had left my job. I had wanted a little time to adjust to the change in my life. As I've told you, the great love which we'd had for each other had slowly expired. The last few years of our marriage had felt a little empty.

I still did my freelance work until quite recently.

I look at my life and I am happy. It's been a life, a real life, and thanks to Second-Phase it never ended in death.

I was always a great animal lover. I had dogs in my life on Earth. I remember my beloved Sasha, who we had got from Battersea Dogs Home when I had been twelve.

Yet in Second-Phase, there are no animals. Just people and robotic programs which imitate animals. I knew that I would want a real pet once I was back on Earth.

Chapter Four

The day finally came when I was to leave my life in Second-Phase and enter a new life on Earth, in London.

The office which I entered was clear and white. The lady at the desk was a real employee and not a robot.

'Good morning,' she said.

'Hi. I'm just preparing to enter Earth. I've got my paperwork.'

'What's your name please?'

'Anita Connell.'

'Ah, yes. All your paperwork's cleared. You've seen the psychiatrists; doctors' checks have been done on your body. Ah, I see you're using your own DNA for the body, that's lovely. Well, just sit over there, Anita, and my colleague will take you into the room where you'll be prepared.'

'Thank you,' I said, as I took my seat.

I took a magazine from the table. 'Vouge Freedom' read the cover, 'year 2419 December'. I looked through last year's December Vouge from Freedom. I enjoy looking through the beautiful fashions and the gorgeous models. On this occasion I didn't recognise any of them, as I'm not really into fashion.

After forty minutes, the administrator came out. She was a pretty black woman who looked to be in her twenties.

'Hi, Anita, come this way,' she said.

I followed her into her office. She was holding a scanning device on her phone and had a sleek laptop on the desk. I sat opposite her.

'Right, Anita. You have one last option to change your mind. Should you change your mind, be aware you'll need to wait another year to apply.'

'No, it's fine. I'm ready to go back to Earth.'

'How exciting,' she said with a smile. 'OK. Here is your ID card, which will be next to you in your bag of things when you wake up in your body.

You will be assigned a guide, just the same as you were when you entered Second-Phase.'

'Yes,' I said.

The administrator looked through my files one more time. She had met me before when I applied to re-enter Earth; her name is Denise.

'So, going back to London, where your life began,' Denise observed.

'Yes, I think it will be a good place to start,' I said.

'OK. Just place your finger on the tablet and you will leave Second-Phase,' Denise said.

I felt my hands tremble as I was about to touch the tablet. I looked at Denise, who smiled calmly. I reached out and placed my hand on the tablet.

I felt myself teleport just how I would normally. Yet then a feeling of blackness took over me. I heard a voice that I was expecting from the inductions about leaving Second-Phase.

'You are now leaving Second-Phase and entering Northwick Park Hospital in the year 2420, the day is April 20th. It is a Sunday, and the weather is mild,' said the computer voice.

I gasped as I breathed in air. I felt the oxygen rush into my lungs, yet it felt more nervous than the steady air I was used to. I opened my eyes and looked at my hands. I saw the slender olive skin of the body of my twenties. Only a little younger than I'd been for so long.

I breathed in deeply. I'd made it. I was back on Earth.

*****

I sat up on the hospital bed; there were a few little instruments attached to me with flashing lights. I didn't touch them. I looked around me at the ultra-modern hospital room.

A nurse with her hair tied in a bun smiled at me. 'Lie back please' she whispered.

I did as she said and lay on the hospital bed.

'You've just woken up?' she asked.

'I'm here on Earth?' I felt the sound of my voice and how I sounded just the same as I always have.

'Yes, you're fine. I guess it's quite scary coming back. Just lie back. We keep everyone in hospital for a few days before they can go to their new life,' said the nurse. 'Anita Connell ... I can get you some water if you want?'

'OK, thanks.'

The nurse walked over to the water tank and got me some water in a plastic cup. She walked back and handed me the water.

'You can sit up now.'

I sat up and the hospital bed adjusted to my sitting position. I looked around to see there was no one else in the other beds in the hospital wing.

'You're from London?' asked the nurse.

I took a sip of my water. 'Yes, I grew up in Edgware. We moved to Beckton in East London when I was fourteen.'

'Ah, OK. So, you're back now. A hundred years is a long time. Have you been keeping up with the news on Earth?' I saw that her name tag read Asuka.

'Yes, I kept up with the news on Earth. It's amazing how much peace Second-Phase brought to the world.'

'Yes, it really is wonderful. War is now just a thing in history books,' Asuka said, beaming at me. She was a short woman of Asian heritage, with medium-length hair.

'So, is this ward just for people re-entering Earth?'

'Yeah. There's not many people coming back to Harrow! Yet every major hospital has to have a ward for this. Your guide will come by tomorrow and allocate you somewhere to live. State benefits are still the same as you will have known.'

'That's great,' I said. I was informed I could have a micro-flat or be assigned a council property. I could also rent privately and the state would pay my rent until I was working.

'Do you want the TV on?' Asuka asked.

'Sure.'

'If you need anything, just give me a shout,' Asuka said, as she sat on her desk at the front of that small area of the hospital.

I had the remote to the TV, which moved in front of my bed and was a small twenty-inch flat screen. I wouldn't have my phone until the next day, yet I was happy to just watch a little bit of TV.

I watched the news on the local channel for Harrow, which is run by the local newspaper. It was night-time. The news was being read by two young people in their twenties. They described local events going on.

'A young woman has set up a local charity to help people deal with anxiety,' read the female newsreader.

'What a great person she is,' said the male newsreader, 'watch this video.'

The news report showed an interview with a woman who looked to be in her forties with long, curly hair. The woman being interviewed talked about how even though acute mental illnesses can be cured by medicine, people still suffer from things such as anxiety. She had started the charity to create a sense of community and to raise money for people to get involved in helping each other.

Asuka brought me a decaf coffee and we talked. I asked her about her job. She told me she had been a nurse for ten years. She explained how she'd come originally from China and that that's where she had studied. Her first language was Mandarin but she had learnt English fluently from school.

She sat with me for a while and I told her about my life before Second-Phase. I told her how I had a sister called Bethanie. She asked me if I'd miss Second-Phase. I explained that I would, but since divorcing my husband, I needed a new experience.

I didn't tell her how my husband had gone to live on Veranna to bring up a child. Yet I enjoyed talking a little with her. We talked for about an hour.

'You woke up at a late time. I can call the guide tomorrow if you're tired and get her to come later.'

'Maybe. I'll try and get some rest,' I said.

Asuka lowered the lights in the ward around me and closed my curtain. With the TV off and her sitting on her desk, I lay in the hospital bed and tried to sleep.

The bed was comfortable, and my body felt great. I felt fit enough that I could have run a mile or taken a dance class. I was limitlessly fit in Second-Phase, as all people are, yet on Earth a body has its limits.

I eventually fell asleep as I remembered things and my mind simply got bored of thinking. When I woke up, it was 11 a.m.

'Good morning,' said a new nurse who had blonde hair in a high pony-tail. 'Asuka's shift is over, so I'll get you ready for meeting your guide,' she said; her name tag read Dianna.

'Thank you,' I said.

Dianna asked me if I wanted breakfast. I agreed, as my body felt hungry, a sensation that doesn't really belong to Second-Phase. Food is more for enjoyment, as there isn't the same bodily requirement of nourishment.

Dianna asked me what I wanted from a hospital menu. I asked for tea and toast. She typed the order into her tablet. Shortly after, a dinner lady brought my food into the room on a plastic tray.

The woman who brought my breakfast looked to be in her fifties, and she appeared healthy and happy. She smiled at me as she handed me the tray.

I smiled back as she left. I ate my food and asked Dianna what time my guide would be coming. Dianna said it was up to me, as the guide wouldn't have any other clients for the day.

I asked to get my things and then I would decide. Dianna asked me if I wanted a shower and I agreed that would be nice.

There was a shower room on the ward. I was given clean towels and a dressing gown. I had already picked the clothes I wanted to wear on my first day from a catalogue when I was in Second-Phase. I had picked a black tracksuit and a pair of white trainers. Dianna handed me the size ten clothes and the size five shoes.

The wash pack contained a bar of soap, shower gel and loafer from The Body Shop. It was in a strawberry scent.

I turned the shower on and the hot water flowed over my body. I had also been given a generic shampoo and conditioner. I hadn't heard of the brand before. I washed my body first and felt how slender I was. I was slimmer than I was when I was thirty.

I washed my long, thick brown hair and placed the conditioner on the ends. As I showered, I thought about where I wanted to live. I'd have to decide that when the guide got there.

After the shower, I dried my hair quickly, before getting into my outfit. I was on my own in the shower area and looked in the mirror. I was pretty, with dark olive skin and bright brown eyes. My hair was very long, as I had requested my hair to look that way. I was just how I wanted to be for a new life.

Once I was dressed, I left the room and re-entered the main hospital ward I was in.

Dianna explained to me how the government had given me my first month's payment of state benefits. It was £2,500.

'The minimum state benefit is about twenty-five thousand a year,' Dianna said, 'but the government will work out your rate if and when you choose to go back to work.'

'Great,' I said, as I took my bank card.

'What phone shall I pick up for you? All your data and stuff will be applied to it, so you'll have all your contacts from Second-Phase,' Dianna said with a smile.

'I've always gone with Samsung, so I'll pick them,' I said.

Dianna showed me the latest Samsung phones that were available in the local Argos, which my guide would pick up for me. I picked a model which cost £150. I'd been away from Earth so long that phone technology had improved exponentially, yet it was always fantastic technology to begin with.

'Right. They have seven colours in stock,' Dianna said, 'any preference?'

I picked a black model of the sleek Samsung which was part of their more budget-friendly phone lines. I knew how much things cost in the real world, yet my flat in Second-Phase cost £1; it would be funny comparing prices to how much things were in Second-Phase's ultra-micro economy.

'I'll order it for you now and take it out of your money, just swipe here,' Dianna said, as she placed a small tablet in front of me where an NHS app was open.

I swiped my new card, which had my state benefit on it. The card pinged and read out that £150 had been taken out for a pay-as-you-go-ready Samsung phone with one million terabytes.

'Not a bad phone,' Dianna said with a smile.

'Yes, indeed. I imagine phones have improved a lot. I've seen technology shows like *Tech Talk*,' I said.

Dianna informed me that my guide Cheryl would be there in an hour's time. Dianna got me a can of caffeine-free diet coke on my request from the vending machine inside the hospital.

The woman in her fifties brought the coke, as Dianna had to stay and keep an eye on me until I left the hospital.

All my vitals were fine, and my mind was sharp. I was ready to start my adventure living on Earth, there in London in the year 2420.

Cheryl looked about forty; she was short with curly blonde hair and was wearing fashion glasses.

'Hi, I'm Cheryl Brown, your guide for the next few weeks while you assimilate back into life on Earth.'

'Hi, thank you.'

Cheryl explained that I needed accommodation. She told me there were vacant flats available for rent which had short leases, so if I moved, I could simply alter the lease on my online paperwork.

She explained that with council property, I'd need to stay in a temporary flat, which could also be arranged. Modern council housing was excellent, yet I wanted to move around, so I decided it wasn't for me.

I decided to take up a three-month let on a one-bedroom flat behind the park that sat behind the main station in Harrow. The flat was ultra-modern. The rent would be paid by my housing benefit, so I wouldn't have to worry about it costing me any of my income.

'Great. It looks a lovely flat. Are you sure, as I'm just about to finalise it,' she said, as she held her white tablet in her hands.   'Yes, it looks beautiful,' I said.

'That's great. Here's to your new home,' she said, pressing her finger down on the app's 'rent' button and then asking me to do the same. 'The property's fully furnished and your fingerprint will open the door. I'm going to print you off some keys with your fingerprint as well, as most people like that.'

'Thank you,' I replied, smiling at Cheryl.

Cheryl explained that the state gave everyone a free basic model of driverless car. Mine was waiting outside for me; it looked like a white bubble, with wheels and a control panel for the computer to drive us.

It had the capacity for two people to sit in the car – me and Cheryl – as it was a basic economy model for a single person. Cheryl sat next to me and I looked at the car.

I had a driverless car in my real life before Second-Phase; I could remember that my car was one which was much fancier than this one. I smiled to myself thinking of the car. I knew that the car was not a flying model, so I couldn't go on holiday with it, yet I thought that I might upgrade in the future.

The car drove us from the hospital to the car park outside the block of blue flats which I was now to live in. The journey took ten minutes. Cheryl talked about how the flat was fully furnished, with the basics such as a fridge, television, etc.

'You'll just need to buy a new computer, or you know there's state-given ones. Could have done the same with your phone, but it's nice to have a fancier model,' Cheryl said with a smile.

'For now, I'll just have a state-funded laptop and tablet. I want to use my money wisely.

Everything costs so much more than in Second-Phase.'

'Do you want a small or larger screen laptop?' Cheryl asked.

'A small screen will be perfect.'

Cheryl explained that she would order them in a minute and bring them around later that day.

I walked to the high-rise blue building and entered my flat, which was number forty-six in the building. The key with my fingerprint opened the door. Cheryl and I stepped foot into my newly rented property.

It had been decorated in neutral colours. It was a one-bedroom flat. There was a shower cubicle in the bathroom that was empty of soaps and other commodities I'd need.

The heating panel looked simple to use outside of the bathroom. The hallway was bright and as we walked into the kitchen, I saw there was a microwave, cooker, fridge-freezer, etc. all there for my use. All the items looked clean and modern.

In the living room, the floor was carpeted grey. The walls were white and there was a large black sofa and two armchairs. There was a window that overlooked the park. I could see people playing outside in the park.

'There's a college right by the flat,' Cheryl said, 'just a minute's walk from the park.'

I expressed how that was nice. She asked me if I would do a course there. I told her that I have a bachelor's degree from the University of East London in Art. I also did an AI bachelor's degree accredited from the University of East London in Computer Science. Not to mention the diploma I got in my afterlife in Second-Phase, which was in Graphic Design.

'I love the AI degree,' Cheryl said with a smile. 'The technology has improved so much. It's a good way to train in something new for a small fee. Employers really value an AI degree.'

'Yes,' I agreed, beaming.

AI degrees run on a computer-generated program, where the whole degree has been designed by artificial intelligence. Most universities run AI degrees in almost every field. Unlike a human-taught bachelor's or master's, etc., an AI degree will state that it was an 'AI bachelor's degree accredited by sed university' on the certificate.

All your professors at an AI degree are made from virtual reality and are not real people. Yet the programming means they look real enough to you. It's a great way to continue education. I got a 2:2 in my AI degree in Computer Science.

Cheryl asked me if I wanted to get some food for my home. We decided to order a delivery. She got out her tablet and asked me what groceries I wanted. I explained how I just wanted a basic order of some ready meals, sweets and tea, etc.

We placed the order, which cost £40. We ordered from Tesco. We got confirmation that a delivery robot named Malcolm would be delivering the food in two hours' time.

Cheryl handed me my new Samsung phone, which she had picked up from Argos before collecting me from the hospital. She inserted the sim. It had a dual sim, so all my contacts from Second-Phase were able to contact me, yet I also had a fresh number on the phone for my new life.

As she handed me the sleek black phone, I signed into my Google Play account, which would mean all the books and music I'd ever bought would also be on my phone.

'Shall we order some lunch?' Cheryl asked.

We ordered some lunch from a local burrito restaurant. The food came within twenty minutes and was delivered by a delivery robot. The human-like robot smiled at us as we took our food and wished us a good day.

We both had vegetarian burritos with tofu and salad inside them. I had a can of Coke and she had a coffee in a plastic cup.

'I've been meaning to ask you,' Cheryl said, 'I got an email about the Harrow Historical Society. You're the only person in the area who has lived in Second-Phase, so to speak, and now is a re-entered citizen.' She smiled and her eyes were warm.

'Oh?'

'Yes, well they'd like to interview you for a book that will be published in next year's magazine. They won't probe you with questions you don't want to answer. Yet they'd like to know about your life in London two hundred years ago and also your experiences in Second-Phase.'

I thought about the prospect of being interviewed for a book. It sounded exciting.

'It sounds interesting,' I said.

'Shall I give the journalist your contact details? The name of the young journalist in charge of the interviews is Finn Mcgonagle,' Cheryl said.

I agreed and she said she would let the Harrow Historical Society know that Finn could interview me. She explained how once the book was finished, they would give me £5,000.

I thought of how I might go on a really interesting holiday with the money. I could even be fancy and take a plane instead of a flying car!

After we ate our food, my laptop and tablet soon arrived, delivered by a robot from the council. Cheryl and I took the items and I left them on a small coffee table by the sofa.

They were sleek models, yet not the latest and greatest technology, as they were free from the council. Yet they were a brand-new laptop and tablet. They were simply twenty years old in the versions of Windows and Android which they ran. Everyone was awarded state staple gadgets such as a phone, laptop and tablet as part of government policy around the world.

Once I had unpacked my food from Tesco, there wasn't much more to say. Cheryl explained that I could call her any time, as she didn't have any clients until I was signed off.

She had already put her number in my phone and there was a picture of her on the icon.

Cheryl wished me farewell and explained that she'd see me the next week. She notified me that Finn would be in touch to discuss the interviews over the next few months.

I was alone in my flat. I was glad I had a week's groceries all packed away in my kitchen.

I posted a picture of my new flat on my Facebook profile. I had 5,600 friends on Facebook, yet when someone's lived in two realities and clocked up over two hundred years, it's understandable one would have met a lot of people.

I decided I would message Charlotte soon. It would be great to meet up with her in Camden. I looked young and I knew she looked stunning with her new black hair and petite body that she had picked.

I spent the rest of the day watching television. I watched the news. The Labour Party was currently in power and would continue to be for another four years before the next general election.

In the world, every country has a living wage and high benefits. Even the so-called 'poor' are very comfortable. There is no poverty in the world and people flourish creatively.

Science is one of the biggest-paying jobs a person can go into, yet artists are valued greatly and the arts are booming with wonderful talent.

The education system hasn't changed much since I was alive. All education around the world is free from school age to PhD level.

AI education has branched out into schooling. When I was alive, it was only for university-level education. Yet now, it supplements even school teaching. Young children can have AI tutors which cost very little.

The world is a beautiful place. I am happy to live in these wonderful times, where science has liberated the human race and we are travelling into the universe to live on other planets such as Veranna. The five habitable planets will mark the next step in human history.

I ordered ten journals and some pens from The Works. I picked pretty diaries with nice covers. The delivery for my order confirmed that a robot would deliver the items within an hour.

I think it's important to write things down. I thought I could start by compiling the memories of my life. I could give the journals to Finn. I decided that I must remember that when I was writing them. I would not mention my ex-husband Michael in great detail. Yet I would mention him a little, as I knew he would want honesty within the book that Finn would be writing.

By 7 p.m., I decided to go for a walk. I walked through the park and through the train station to get into the main town. The station was modern like I remembered it, full of blue interior and lightning-fast trains.

Outside, the train station had a flying car taxi rank. The drivers were real people who were sitting in their cars. I looked at their black cars and smiled to myself, imagining them going abroad or simply flying to another town.

I crossed the road and walked through the shopping centre. I'd already ordered my groceries and washing essentials, yet I needed some clothes to fill the wardrobe. I could order some, yet I decided to enter a clothing shop.

I went into Primark, which was a little busy but not madly packed. The clothes in there were cheap, made by robots. I looked around at the beautiful clothes. I picked up a red raincoat and some leggings. I also took a few T-shirts.

As I entered the female changing room, I changed into the new outfit. I felt beautiful and looked good in the size ten clothes that I had selected.

Changing back into my tracksuit, I queued up. The people in the queue all looked different. There was a woman with a very extravagant hairstyle. No one paid attention to anyone and the queue moved quickly.

The checkout staff were mainly real people and some were robots. The one that served me was a human – I knew this as it said on her name tag. My coat, two pairs of leggings and two T-shirts came to £55. I paid for the items with my card and placed it back in the little black bag I had.

When I left the shop, it was almost closing time. I exited the shopping centre which was soon to close. I didn't grow up in Harrow but I know the area well. The shops had changed yet a lot of them were still the same.

Waterstones lay opposite the shopping centre. It was full of paperback books from the latest and greatest best-selling, traditionally published authors. I noticed they had a small table for indie authors as I looked outside from the window.

I walked through the town, thinking it would be nice to go to a café and have a tea. I noticed a milkshake bar as I walked through town. I entered it and ordered a strawberry milkshake.

    I sat alone with my drink on a small table. My phone beeped; it was an email from Finn. He had introduced himself. The email told me a little about him and his career so far as a journalist. He had worked for Harrow's historical centre since graduating from university. He had sent a picture of himself; he was quite handsome, with high cheekbones and straight blond hair.

    We arranged through emails to meet later in the week. I felt excited to start the experience.

    When I got home, the delivery of my journals was there along with the pens. I opened my door and settled in. I thought about how I should start writing the story of my life.

Chapter Five

Before my next meeting with Cheryl, which was on Saturday, I had time for myself. I took another shopping trip to Watford. I got the Metropolitan Line, which zoomed through each station at lightning speed. The train was modern and clean.

I got off at Watford, which had a bigger shopping centre than Harrow did. I looked around at the markets, which sold unique pieces from fashion designers in the local proximity.

I picked up a beautiful coat from a fashion graduate whose stall was called 'Ella's Designs'. The coat was green, with black hearts. It had a fake leather tie in the middle and big black buttons. I tried on the coat, picking up a size ten from the rack.

'Hey, you look great in my design,' said the owner of the stall.

I paid for the coat, which cost £60. She put it in a bag which featured her logo.

I then got a few tops from chain shops in the major shopping centre. When I got home, I took the train once more, using my card to pay for the journey.

I hung up my new coat in my wardrobe, which was slowly becoming full of clothes. I had two coats and a collection of jeans and tops for the spring.

It was late in April. The weather was sweet and the air was fresh. I have always enjoyed this time of year.

I was to meet with Charlotte the following week. She had rented a large, one-bedroom property in a complex in Camden. She had shown me pictures on WhatsApp.

'Soon to be joining a local dramatic society. It will be so nice to meet some new people. You know, I really want to make it as an actress in a different way than I did before,' Charlotte typed, as she showed me a picture of the arts centre building where she would be partaking in local plays.

Charlotte had a degree in Drama from Chicago, which was where she had lived in her life before Second-Phase. As you recall in her life on Earth, her body had been small and not the most attractive.

She had taught Drama to high school students in America. She had also narrated many audiobooks. Yet she had always dreamed of being an actress for film and television; she had wanted to play the glamorous roles of the beauty queens.

In Second-Phase, she had been able to achieve this dream. She had been in a lot of independent films. The art industry in Second-Phase is unending. She was a brilliant actress and I had watched one film which she had been in.

Yet now she was in a third guise; she no longer looked like the blonde actress in the films she had appeared in within her afterlife in Second-Phase, or the short and small woman she had been in life who had taught high school drama.

Now Charlotte had taken on a new, beautiful body with long black glossy hair and bright blue eyes. She had been back on Earth for as long as myself. Everyone in the year 2420, who re-entered Earth from Second-Phase, was part of the generation who entered on that amazing day in April.

We had purple Facebooks and our ID tags indicated we were from that generation. We had all the same rights as every citizen, yet we were part of a new generation, leaving Second-Phase to live in the world once more.

I was looking forward to seeing Charlotte. We were going to catch up on everything that was going on in our lives. I guessed I would hear all about the play she was rehearsing for. I could tell her about the life I hoped to build in Harrow.

*****

When I met with Cheryl, she asked me what I had been doing with myself. I explained that I had joined the local gym, which was in the shopping centre.

'That's fantastic,' she said with a smile. 'Are you excited about the book?'

'I am,' I said.

Cheryl asked me what I planned to do and if I wanted to stay on benefits or look for a job. I was on the lowest amount for state benefits, which was £25,000 a year. Yet I was living well on that.

'I'm going to stay at this flat for the three months. I will let Finn interview me for the book and really give him all the information to write a great book. Yet afterwards, I think I'd like to travel. I think I'll take a flying car or maybe even a plane and I will go abroad for a holiday.'

'Fantastic. Where will you go?' Cheryl asked, smiling.

'I don't know yet. Somewhere I've never visited before.'

Cheryl explained that I could extend my lease for up to five years whenever I wanted. I hadn't yet decided if I'd move. I knew I wanted to travel but didn't know yet if I'd stay in England. For now, three months sounded like a good amount of time to live in the nice flat.

Cheryl handed me an information pack about the modern world. It consisted of a few leaflets containing facts about society, and I would most definitely look at them later.

As Cheryl left, she told me that the next time she would see me would be in two weeks' time.

She explained that I was to email if I needed to speak to her sooner.

When she went, I ordered a Chinese takeaway from my Just Eat app. The delivery robot would be delivering my food within an hour.

I looked at the diary that I had filled for Finn to read; the diary would help him write the book.

I had described how I lived in Edgware and how we moved to Beckton when I was fourteen. I explained how I was a young person in the early 2200s. Second-Phase was new then and although it had been around for a generation, I was part of the first few generations to enter it when I grew old.

I would speak with my grandmother through a VR headset. She died when I was twelve. I remember being so sad, yet knowing that she was still alive in the digital world had brought me so much joy. My grandmother who died was on my mother's side and had been born in Delhi. She had moved to England in her twenties to study Photography at university.

I remember how my gran had been a great photographer. She spoke with an accent and wanted me to learn Gujarati, yet I never did. She was a kindly grandmother who loved animals. She was a great cook and was a talkative woman. She always had good advice for me.

My surname Connell came from my mother's side of the family. My grandad was from Ireland. He was an architect. He lived in London yet was originally from Dublin in Ireland.

I wrote about how my experiences as a child were influenced by spending time with my grandmother, visiting her in VR as she lived her afterlife in Second-Phase. I described the beautiful home she kept in the digital reality. How she would always love hearing what me and Bethanie had been up to at high school.

My grandmother was thrilled when I chose GCSE Art. She helped me with art – after all, she had a bachelor's degree in Photography. She taught me about perspective and the study of art in rich detail.

I then went on, aged sixteen, to study a BTEC in Fine Art. I also took an A Level in Psychology, which meant I had a lot of UCAS points by the time I was prepared to apply for university.

I described how I was shy with boys. I got attention from boys and compliments, yet I didn't have my first proper boyfriend until I was eighteen and had finished my college studies.

His name was Rodrigo, and he was good-looking with black hair and green eyes. Our connection was weird. We liked each other probably because we found each other good-looking, yet we weren't right for each other. We dated for three months and although we were happy at times, the romance fizzled out.

I remember being sad when I broke up with Rodrigo. We kept in touch as friends for quite some years after, until we lost contact altogether.

I described in my journal how I then took a year out before my studies at the University of East London. By this time, Bethanie had left for Liverpool Hope University, where she was to study Accounting.

Bethanie was staying in halls of residence on the campus in Liverpool. I remember seeing the pictures of my pretty sister with the new friends that she had made. It was nice, seeing her do well.

I might not have mentioned this before but Bethanie and I are non-identical twins. We share the same birthday of 5 August.

She was at university and no longer living at home. Bethanie had taken some of her things with her to university, yet her room in our family house still held a lot of her clothes and drawings on the wall.

Our dog Sasha would sometimes go into Bethanie's room. Sasha was a beautiful Collie mongrel who loved to say woof. Bethanie and I both loved our dog, as did our parents.

I described in my diary how I had worked at a clothing shop called Monsoon for the year out before starting at the University of East London.

We still lived in Beckton and I had planned to study there, so I would not have to live on campus. I wanted to hang out with my friends who lived locally.

My room in the semi-detached house we had in Beckton was quite big. It was in the middle of the house. My dog would sit on the bed while I sat on my sofa.

I enjoyed working in Monsoon. I wore beautiful clothes from their shop as part of my work uniform. I was fairly good at my job. It was before robots were doing a lot of jobs.

I saved a lot of money that year. When I started my Art degree the following September, I wore a designer coat to my induction. It was from Chanel and had cost me £500. No one noticed it was designer, yet another student commented on how nice my coat was.

I wrote about my studies in Fine Art. I was at the university for three years and graduated with a 1st aged twenty-two.

I then went on to work in London for a while. I worked in an office job. I moved out of home and rented a micro-flat in the city. The rent was cheap and I liked the minimalism of it. I still visited my family in Beckton.

I talked about how I met Michael at an alumni event that I went to in my thirties. I was doing an AI bachelor's degree from the University of East London in Computer Science. I was doing a foundation year before starting the three-year degree. My studies were wholly virtual, and all my professors were holograms.

When I met Michael, he had been a master's student at the University of East London. He was studying Physics. He was originally from Devon. He was smart and fairly good-looking, yet there was a beauty that shone so bright from his smart and kind personality.

I had found him so easy to talk to. So interesting and fun. The way his face lit up with our first conversation. I had been brave and asked for his number.

Two years later, we were married and living together. I wrote all this down in the diary. The pages were full of my neat handwriting, telling the history of my life and the emotions I felt. I talked about the times and how Second-Phase had shaped a world. The fear of death had gone.

Yet the world was changing dramatically, too. We were in the age where world peace was truly accomplished.

My Chinese food arrived as I put the diaries in my bag. I was to meet with Finn the next day. I hoped that he wasn't a shark of a journalist, but from his email he sounded friendly. It sounded like the book was intended to simply be a way of understanding someone's account of leaving Second-Phase and re-entering Earth.

Chapter Six

Finn met me in Harrow. He was wearing a black vest top and grey jeans. He was slender and had high cheekbones. He had perfect teeth. He had his phone in his hands. When he saw me enter the milkshake bar we had arranged to meet in, he smiled.

'Anita, hi,' Finn said.

I sat opposite him and he half-smiled.

'It's a pleasure to meet you,' Finn said.

He put his phone on the table. His eyes were blue like the sea and his hair was a sandy blond. He told me about the book he would be writing, how it would be part of the Harrow Historical Society's annual book that it writes for the magazine.

'The book will be free in next year's edition of the magazine,' Finn said. 'After that edition, it will go on sale online, are you OK with that?'

'Sure,' I said.

He explained that the year's edition was about historical events in Harrow. It was written about migration patterns and how last year Finn had interviewed historians and anthropologists.

'Great. Well, let me explain my part in all of this. Over the next month or so, if it is OK with you, I will be interviewing you. If you could send me some pictures for the book, I'd really appreciate that, too.'

'Of course,' I said with a smile.

I handed Finn the diary which I had completed about my life. I explained to him how it contained some of the stories he could focus on when writing about me for the book.

'Oh, that is fantastic, you're a star, Anita,' he said. His eyes lit up as his slender hands held the diary.

Finn and I talked for a while. He told me how he was a Journalism graduate, and how he had done a bachelor's degree in Journalism at the Harrow campus of the University of Westminster.

He had been working writing articles for the Harrow Historical Society for a year. He explained how he loved history.

'It explains so much about humanity,' Finn said.

I smiled and he smiled back. His smile lines were very present on his slender face. He looked like a catalogue model.

'So, what are your plans after the book is out?' Finn asked me.

'I think I'll travel once it's out. I will be sure to read it. It will be interesting to read how I am written about.'

Finn asked me where I would travel to. I explained that I didn't know. I was thinking of taking a plane to another country as opposed to travelling by flying car. Planes had developed and were much more of a luxury than a flying car.

'But flying cars are practically free,' said Finn with a laugh. 'Well, I can imagine flying in a plane is very luxurious.'

Finn told me how he was originally from Dublin. He moved to England when he enrolled on his Journalism degree. He told me how he had brought his dog Misty with him.

'Do you live on your own with your dog?' I asked, feeling my question might be a bit prying.

Yet Finn simply smiled, with a calmness in his expression. 'Well, Misty is enough company for one person. She is my world. Would you like to see a picture of her?'

I said that I would love to see a picture of his dog. He went on to tell me how she was expecting puppies. He explained how he would get her neutered after the litter, yet he had felt it would be nice to breed a small litter of Westies.

'She's expecting four healthy pups,' Finn said with a smile, showing me a photo of the pregnant West Highland Terrier.

'Ah, that is lovely. Will you keep any of them?'

'Oh no. Misty is the only girl for me. We have already got new homes lined up for them. The birth should be easy; we have booked a robotic vet to be on call, and you know they're more foolproof than a human one anyway. I've met with the prospective owners, too. All of them are lovely people.'

Finn went on to tell me that he wasn't going to charge the people for the Westie puppies. He was a member of a breeding website which ethically made sure dogs went to good homes.

'Do you have one of those dog-walking robots?' I asked.

'Oh, yeah. She's only a little lass so it's just a short thing. I've never used it, though; I think they are great. You know how they can protect the dog and all. But she loves me taking her on walkies.'

'They didn't have dog-walking robots when I was young, before I entered Second-Phase,' I said.

'Were you a dog owner in your first life?'

'We had quite a few dogs over the years,' I said. 'I'll send you pictures of them if you like, how long will the book be?'

'It depends. We're aiming for anywhere between 20,000 and 150,000 words,' Finn said with a laugh. 'My Journalism degree will be paying for itself.'

'Well, I'll do my best to create an interesting account of the times and my life,' I said, beaming.

'So, is it really just like living and breathing on Earth, Second-Phase?' Finn said, raising an eyebrow quizzically.

'Yes. You can taste the food, feel the texture of the sand on your feet. Yet you cannot feel pain and your body does not have the physical constraints. You do feel tiredness, though, unless you modify that out of your body with a doctor's procedure.'

'Fascinating,' Finn said with a sigh. 'I'm going to live my best life here and now. When I one day get there, please God let it be a long time from now, I'll really miss having dogs.'

I agreed with him that I missed having real animals. Robotic simulations weren't the same. I did sometimes like to have a pretend dog around just to watch it play with other dogs on the beach. I didn't tell him this, yet I remembered doing that over several years.

'I sponsor the Dogs Trust,' he said, beaming. 'I donate 1 per cent off all my money to them.'

'You love dogs,' I said with a smile.

Finn went on to talk more about the Dogs Trust. He must have been on good money. I knew I was on the lowest wage a single person in the UK could have and yet I was still very comfortable.

He explained how the Dogs Trust rehome dogs who are given to them. They have a great social media presence. All the dogs that can be rehomed are always rehomed. He explained if a dog could not be rehomed, they would still make its life wonderful through dog-walking robots and other things to help give them a good quality of life.

He asked me if I wanted a milkshake. He ordered what I asked for and got himself a coffee. We talked for another hour. He explained how he would send me a questionnaire the next day of certain things that he would need to know for the book.

'Do you want a lift home? You didn't bring your car,' Finn said.

'Oh, no. I live a few minutes away. Are you far from here?'

'Just Stanmore, it isn't far. I'll get a bus,' Finn said, as he waved goodbye to me.

As I walked home, I thought how charming and genuinely nice he seemed. He was a breath of fresh air to talk with. I really enjoyed his company.

When I was home, I looked up his social media. He was indeed a budding journalist, yet his articles were all really positive and there didn't seem to be a cut-throat style to his writing.

I had a microwavable meal of a vegetarian curry. After my meal, I looked through my state computer. It had the same amount of memory as my phone. I had access to all the files from my

Cloud account that I had created on previous computers.

I looked through an old file, which contained pictures from when I was at university studying Art. I was young, like I am now. Yet the London I lived in was not so technologically as advanced back then. There were not robots working in shops that looked like humans.

The human race was becoming immortal in Second-Phase, yet it was not living on other planets such as Veranna, Sueno, Helena, Vex and Twilight.

It made me think of Michael and how he was on his way to Veranna. I allowed myself to include a few photographs of him from his late thirties, when he had met me, in the file that I would send Finn for the book. I explained how my ex-husband was of the generation that would form the first community to live on the habitable planet of Veranna.

Chapter Seven

The next day, I fired up my laptop and went through the questionnaire that Finn had sent me. I took an hour to answer the questions in detail. When I emailed him the answers, I felt strange.

It had been two lifetimes. One on Earth and another in Second-Phase, and now there I was in the same body. Yet Michael was gone and I no longer loved him.

So, who would I love this time? I thought about my sexuality. I'd only ever slept with two men in my life. One was Michael and before that there had been a short-lived boyfriend called Blake.

Blake had been a calm lover and had greatly excited me with lust. Yet our relationship had burnt out quickly. I didn't regret that it hadn't worked out because two years later I had met Michael and he had been my everything for so long.

I did not know how I felt about exploring my sexuality in this new life I'd been allowed to have. I knew why I'd come to Earth once more; I wanted children. Michael and I had decided against it when we had been together. It simply had not been part of our path as a couple in the times we had lived in.

Yet when I thought about how happy Bethanie was to be a mother of two beautiful girls, I saw that my nieces had given her such a purpose to her life. I wanted something like that for myself.

I'd been back on Earth for less than a month. It was now May. The weather was warm and the sun shone with such grace in the sky. The park was full of daffodils outside my flat. When I walked through the park, the grass smelt sweet.

I looked through Internet sites for sex shops. The one I knew well was Ann Summers, which had been around for hundreds of years. I looked up sex robots.

I knew that they were fairly expensive, yet I liked the idea. It filled me with excitement to think of feeling what imitated a real man making love to me, knowing that it was just a daydream because the robot would have no thoughts or feelings of his own. Yet his touch would be the same as touching a human.

I ordered a model of a six-foot-two man with large, sleek endowments. The sex robot was a good-looking man with a medium-build sculptured body. I chose this specific model because I found the face and body handsome and well ... he was what they had in stock.

As I paid via PayPal, the order confirmation confirmed that the robot would be delivered later that night at six in the evening.

I set a reminder on my phone. I went out for a walk. I sat in the park on a bench and watched the dogs play and people walk by on their way to the local college.

The fresh warm air felt good against my skin. I was wearing a black pair of leggings and a long top. I had got dolly plimsole shoes on and my hair was flowing loosely around my waist.

I took a selfie on my Samsung phone. Here I was in the year 2420. I made it my new Facebook profile image. I looked pretty.

Almost everyone I knew was in Second-Phase. Bethanie's children had children who were elderly now. They had families of their own. I still had them as contacts on my phone, yet they had their own lives to live. I was not a close enough relative to want to visit them. Not just yet anyway.

I went for lunch at Subway. I had a veggy patty sub and a Pepsi. After lunch, I popped into Primark, where I bought myself some sexy lingerie. I knew that the robot wouldn't care what I looked like, yet he would be programmed to say all the right things.

*****

When I got home that evening, I nervously awaited the delivery robot bringing my sex robot. When the doorbell rang, I hopped up from the sofa to answer it.

The female delivery robot smiled at me and asked me to sign the electronic form with my fingerprint. After doing that, she handed me the black box, which was fairly heavy, and then left.

I closed the door and looked at the box which contained the sex robot. The model had cost me £1,000 and was the cheapest model around.

I'd watched a video on the Ann Summers website about how he could be controlled by my commands. He would make love to me like a mortal man would, whenever I wanted. He was not conscious, though, simply a robot that was designed for my sexual pleasure.

I'd already set the program which came with my user account when I bought the robot. I'd chosen to call the robot Dean. He would answer to that name and was programmed to make love to me after I explicitly explained what I wanted him to do.

I changed into my pink lingerie and silky pants. My slender figure looked so sexy in the mirror. I pressed the button on the box and looked away as the robot unfolded out of his box.

A few minutes later, I heard a ping and turned around to see that a gorgeous resemblance of a man had stepped out of the box. He was wearing white boxers and was erect. I ushered him into the bedroom.

We used lube to get me wet and it smelt of strawberries. The scent turned me on, as did his thorough touching. He breathed heavily, like I'd programmed him to do so.

He made love to me and it felt so good. The softness of his skin was such that it could have belonged to a real man. I moaned in pleasure as I climaxed.

When it was over, I looked at the robot, who was programmed to look at me with a lustful, loving expression.

I asked Dean to clean himself up and then get back into his box.

'As you wish, Anita,' he said, and smiled. I watched him use the wipes that were for hygiene as he cleaned himself.

Continuing to watch him clean his body for a moment, I then left the robot as he entered his box. I listened to him leave the bedroom, where he folded down back into the black box. I heard the beeping noise which meant he was secure and on power save mode in the box, ready to use again whenever I next desired.

I stepped into my shower and washed myself with The Body Shop products I owned. I washed my hair with the Shea butter shampoo and conditioner. My body felt good. It felt so fucking good.

I left the shower and dried myself. I got changed into my pyjamas. I looked at the time; it was only half past seven.

Chapter Eight

Charlotte and I planned to spend the whole day together on Wednesday. She'd invited me to a party in the evening which was being held upstairs at a pub in Baker Street. It was for actors to network.

'Oh, darling, how good it is to see you,' she said, beaming at me.

I was wearing a black dress from Marks & Spencer and a fake pearl necklace. I was also wearing the red raincoat that I had purchased from Primark.

We met at Baker Street Underground Station. I noticed that there was a port outside for flying taxis to take people to holiday destinations.

'Book your hotel online – just take your passport and jet off to wherever you dream of' read the sign outside the flying taxi rank.

Charlotte looked great. Her long black hair was flowing in a glossy mass of perfect waves. Her figure looked like a size eight. She was wearing blue jeans and had on a white denim jacket.

'You look like a film star,' I said with a smile.

Charlotte told me about the party. There would be young and old actors from all around London. It was simply a networking event to make friends. Yet there would be up-and-coming film producers at the party who were always important people to make a good impression with.

Charlotte and I had sushi at a small shop. We sat on the benches and ate our food. I ordered the vegetarian sushi option, even though in the shop's window it was stated that the tuna and salmon had been grown from lab-produced meat.

I enjoyed the avocado and cucumber sushi. I drank a fizzy orange soda with my meal.

'One of the film directors that will be at the party is up-and-coming with the BBC film production company,' Charlotte said. 'He started off making films using AI actors.'

AI actors were the same as AI professors; they only existed in virtual reality. They had no emotions and were simply programmed by humans. In the case of AI actors, it had been a way for people to make extremely low-budget movies on their computers which would have once cost millions of pounds hundreds of years previously.

'What's the name of the film director?' I asked.

'Henry Fitz. I hope he comes and talks to me. I've got my cards printed out ...' Charlotte showed me her cards, which showed a little printout of her profile and her Twitter handle.

We talked about how excited Charlotte was for the party. She told me about the play and how she had got the lead role. She told me how it was a modern twist on *Romeo and Juliet*, which was a famous play in literature by William Shakespeare.

'You'll be one amazing Juliet,' I said, beaming.

Later that evening, we went to the party. We got there early. Charlotte asked that I didn't drink, as it's always important to act professional at such events. I promised her that I've never been much of a drinker anyway and would only have cola.

I enjoyed the party. The actors were confident and talkative. Charlotte introduced me to the actor playing Romeo in the play with her at the Camden Art Centre. He was a good-looking black man.

I talked with the actor playing Romeo with Charlotte. We enjoyed chatting. Soon, the actors started to mingle with other people as the pub got more packed.

Robotic waiters served orders and drinks. I had a Coke and a few mini-sandwiches.

A beautiful man with long black hair and the darkest eyes I'd ever seen approached me. He smiled with a cool confidence.

'Hi,' said the beautiful man.

I blushed and hoped he didn't notice. 'Hi.'

'Are you an actress?' he asked with a smile.

'Oh, goodness no! I'm here with my friend.'

The man introduced himself as Fabio; he told me how he was an actor and looking to make new connections.

'What sort of films are you looking to star in?' I asked.

'Anything. I just want to work, you know,' Fabio said, his expression passionate. 'So, um, what's your name?'

'I'm Anita,' I said.

He asked me about what I do. I felt weird telling him, because I was attracted to him. Yet I explained that I was part of the first generation to leave Second-Phase.

Fabio gasped and then smiled. 'A woman of the school of life.'

We talked for what seemed like a good while. Fabio was thirty-five. He looked younger and he told me how he'd been an actor since he was eighteen. He told me how he'd been in so many independent films, yet he'd never had a big break into stardom.

We really hit it off. He seemed interested to hear about me. He didn't seem bothered when I explained that I was once married and that we had divorced five years previously.

He asked me if I still loved my ex-husband. I told him that we fell out of love and how he went to start a new life on the planet Veranna.

Fabio flirted with me a little more as we continued to talk. He called me beautiful in Italian and asked for my number.

I gave him my phone number and we arranged to go on a date later in the week. Fabio lived in Lewisham in South London. He explained to me how he'd lived there for six months. Before living there, he had been working on an indie film project in Rome, Italy.

When the evening was coming to a close, Fabio wished me a good night. I rejoined with

Charlotte, who had good news. She had made contact with Henry Fitz.

'He said I can audition for his next project!' she said excitedly.

We got the night bus back to her flat in Camden. She'd decorated it with beautiful art.

She pulled out the sofa bed for me to sleep on later. It was extremely comfortable.

We spent some of the night talking. She told me how she dreamt of doing more with acting. She wanted to travel as well.

'That guy you were talking with looked handsome,' Charlotte said, beaming.

I told her about Fabio and how we had planned to go on a date. We had a glass of white wine each and watched a movie with an AI cast and a brilliant script. The film was on an art channel and was a low-budget film, yet it looked so incredibly brilliant.

The film was a thriller and we watched it from start to finish. I enjoyed spending time with Charlotte. She was a kind friend and her company was full of such a lovely energy.

After the movie, I got into the sofa bed and Charlotte went to her room. I slept well and my mind dreamt about the possibilities of a romantic date with Fabio.

The next morning, we went for breakfast at a traditional café. We had fried bread and coffee. We talked about what I should wear for my date.

I then took a driverless taxi back to my flat in Harrow. It was more expensive than the train but I felt lazy. I listened to music on my phone for the twenty-minute drive back to my flat.

When I was home, I napped for a bit before I went to the gym. I looked at the black box with my sex robot Dean inside it. Soon, I might not need to use my sex robot.

Chapter Nine

Fabio and I met for our first date. He had travelled to Harrow in a fancy black driverless Audi car. It wasn't a state-funded model and looked nice.

'It flies,' he explained to me. 'Maybe if we get on well, I'll introduce you to my mother in Rome.'

I asked about his parents. He told me how his mother was the one who he was close with. His father had left his mother when Fabio was five and now had another family. Fabio didn't feel as though he had a father anymore emotionally, he said.

We had a meal at Nando's in the shopping centre. Fabio was wearing a white shirt that complimented his tanned olive skin. He smiled casually as I asked him about his interests.

'Acting … a little modelling. No, but seriously, when I am not working, I enjoy visiting my family.' Fabio's smile was gorgeous.

Fabio didn't seem to ask me many questions, yet made small talk in the form of banter. He joked about things on television and what was currently going on in the media.

'You know, if I wasn't here with you, maybe I should go on *Love Island* to advance my acting career,' Fabio said with a wink.

Love Island was a sexually charged TV series that had been on the television channel ITV for hundreds of years. Each year, men and women who looked like Fabio went on the show to potentially meet someone but more realistically to get a career on television powered by their typical good looks.

I did not feel the connection was deep with Fabio. After the date, we went for a quiet pub drink. Fabio paid most of his attention to me, yet I could see him looking in the direction of other beautiful women at the bar.

When the evening was over, Fabio drove me back to my flat.

'Shall I come in for coffee?' he asked with a wink.

'I'm a little tired. Next time?'

'Yes, baby. Whatever you want,' he said, kissing me softly on the lips.

I left the car and watched him drive off. I thought to myself whether I would call him as I entered my flat. I felt as if he just wanted something heated with me, that at present he was not looking for what I was looking for.

I made myself a cup of tea and checked my emails on my phone as I sat on the sofa. Finn had emailed me. He'd asked if I'd like to meet his dog Misty once the puppies had got their forever homes, once they were old enough. He expressed how he was really enjoying writing the book about me.

I wondered if Finn was asking me on a date? I was too scared to ask him outright, yet I emailed back stating how I'd love to meet Misty.

*****

Well, I never did go on a second date with Fabio. I ended up meeting Finn for a Costa chat instead, as friends. We talked a little on the book, yet more of our conversation was on life in general. He explained that he wouldn't put anything in the book that I told him 'off the record' when meeting with him as 'friends'.

There was obviously an attraction between me and Finn. His catalogue model good looks and kindly face were highlighted in beauty by his wonderful personality.

I adored how much he loved Misty. He was in awe of her puppies. There were three girls and one boy. He had already known the sex of the puppies via a scanning app he had, which had allowed him to know how many puppies Misty was expecting.

'One of the females is going to a family in South London. The other girls are going to Oxfordshire and Hampshire. And the little boy will go to Edinburgh. We are on a special app which means I can see photos of Misty's little family and see how they are doing throughout their lives. It's all part of ethical dog breeding,' Finn said, beaming.

'What's the app called?' I asked.

'My Dog Family Tree,' he said with a smile. 'It has a sister app for cats. Yet there are lots of similar apps that do the same thing.'

He showed me the app and it had a picture of each of the new puppies. The pictures were connected to photos of the families waiting to take them to their forever home. It was really lovely to see how dedicated Finn was to his love of dogs, which is something I share.

*****

I remember how the months passed while Finn interviewed me for the book. We became closer and closer, and soon it was evident that we were falling in love with each other.

When he first asked me on an official date, we had already spent quite a lot of time together. I had video-chatted with him for many of the interviews, seeing the images of his flat in Stanmore, which he lived in with Misty and the four new puppies.

He showed me the dog-caring robot he had, which he rarely used. The little human-shaped robot was small, as Misty was only a little Terrier, yet she liked the robot, as it would give her dog treats.

His flat was full of beautiful fabrics covering the walls of his front room. He had a huge computer screen and a smaller laptop on his desk.

Misty sat in a large dog bed with her puppies, who were full of playful energy. Misty was a calm-natured dog who obviously loved Finn dearly.

He asked me out officially via email. He explained how he wasn't bothered by our age gap and told me that he was fascinated by the wonderful person I was.

I may have been much older than him technically, yet my body was that of a twenty-year-old, with the ensuing fresh vitality. We soon found that our dates became more passionate and that we would end up in my flat, where we would make love.

The first time I made love to Finn was an amazing experience. Just the feeling of being with someone who made me feel beautiful and who I knew liked me for both my looks and personality. I felt whole.

*****

Twenty-six years have passed since the events that I have recalled. I now sit in the house in London which belongs to me and my husband Finn and our daughter Mary.

I have our dog lying on the bed. Whenever I say her name, 'Sandy', the Labrador wags her tail with a lazy happy expression.

Finn and I married one year after we had met. We fell deeply in love and now have an eighteen-year-old daughter. She currently has her hair coloured a bright pink.

Mary is Finn and my pride and joy. She is a beautiful and confident young woman. We are soon moving to Dublin, as Finn wants to go back to Ireland.

Mary is studying a bachelor's degree in Acting in Dublin. She has already aced her audition for the course.

We've bought an old house which was dirt cheap because it's not one of these Google-houses that can be installed by robots. Yet it's beautiful, secure and allows us to have all the necessary mod cons we need to be comfortable.

My body is now that of a forty-six-year-old woman. Finn is soon to celebrate his fifty-second birthday. We are planning on having one more child, yet we've decided that the baby will be carried in an artificial womb. We have already decided that we want another girl.

We are naming the child Diya after my grandmother, who is still very much happy in Second-Phase. My grandmother has a close relationship with her great-granddaughter, my daughter Mary.

I am in contact with Michael. He is happy for me that I have remarried. He has been awake and living in Veranna for a year now. He is part of the first generation of Second-Phase citizens to belong to the habitable planet.

Michael has his baby, who is made from the sperm and egg of a relative of his. He will inform the child about this and how he was unable to be the child's paternal father.

Michael is happy. I see pictures of his baby on Facebook. I see that Michael wants to find love again. He has expressed how he will join a dating site on his planet when his son is old enough. He is happy and he has a fulfilling life as a new father.

The spaceships are still travelling to the four other habitable planets. Sueno is the nearest one. I am excited at the prospect of watching the celebrations in some fifteen years' time, when the first generation will come to the planet, where the robots will be awaiting them. The robots have built the cities and the houses, yet it's the humans that will make the planet a world.

Aliens do exist in the universe, yet they are basic life forms and humans have never discovered anything more intelligent than a fish or mice on other planets. We are the most intelligent form of life in the universe as far as we know.

I visit my family through a VR headset that allows me to view them in Second-Phase. They are all doing different things in the world and experiencing their own lives.

When you've lived as long as we have, you get on with things. One day, I will die and return to

Second-Phase, as will Finn and all the people I love in this world.

I am a mother. I am married to my second husband and expecting my second daughter over the next year. This is my story. The story will continue to go on and on. I do not know if one day Finn and I will fall out of love like I did with Michael. Yet we have a family together and I hope that we can watch the generations go by as we age.

My friend Charlotte made it as a famous actress. Finn interviewed her for a book which he self-published. The book helped grow her fan-base on Twitter.

Charlotte is what one would call a B-list celebrity. She has been in some great films. She has done a lot with her acting career over the last twenty-six years, prior to entering Earth once more. She is a dear and wonderful friend to me. She has been my best friend for many years.

She now lives with her boyfriend Pier in Paris. They have an ultra-modern Google-home that is a particularly luxurious model. She is now fluent in

French. Pier is a dancer and painter. They are so well suited.

I wonder what the future for humanity will bring; will we find more habitable planets? Will we expand our reach to outside the universe? I am not sure of these things, yet humanity lives on Earth and Veranna, and soon we will reach Sueno and the other three planets.

We are in a great age. And that, my friends, is the story of my life so far.

The End

Printed in Great Britain
by Amazon